For Those Just Starting Out . . .

Material from this book originally appeared in
Seuss-isms: Wise and Witty Prescriptions for Living from the Good Doctor,
TM & copyright © by Dr. Seuss Enterprises, L.P. 1997, and
Seuss-isms for Success: Insider Tips on Economic Health from the Good Doctor,
TM & copyright © by Dr. Seuss Enterprises, L.P. 1999, 2009.

Visit us on the Web!
Seussville.com
randomhousekids.com

Educators and librarians, for a variety of teaching tools, visit us at
RHTeachersLibrarians.com

Library of Congress Cataloging-in-Publication Data
Seuss, Dr.
[Poems. Selections]
Seuss-isms! a guide to life for those just starting out . . .
and those already on their way / Dr. Seuss.
pages   cm.
ISBN 978-0-553-50841-3 (trade)
1. Children's poetry, American. 2. Wisdom—Juvenile poetry. 3. Conduct of life. I. Title.
PS3513.E2A6 2015   811'.52—dc23   2014025499

Printed in the United States of America
10 9 8 7 6 5 4 3 2 1
First Edition

Seuss-isms!

A Guide to Life
for Those Just Starting Out . . .
and Those Already on Their Way

By Dr. Seuss

Random House New York

Be True to Yourself

You have brains in your head.
You have feet in your shoes.
You can steer yourself
any direction you choose.
You're on your own. And you know what you know.
And *YOU* are the guy who'll decide where to go.

—*Oh, the Places You'll Go!*

Surround Yourself with Good People

But the YEPS
on the STEPS—
They're great fun
to have around.
And so are
many, many
other friends
that I have found. . . .

—*There's a Wocket in My Pocket!*

Listen to Good Advice

Then he spoke great Words of Wisdom
as he sat there on that chair:
"To eat these things," said my uncle,
"you must exercise great care.
You may swallow down what's solid . . .
BUT . . . you must spit out the air!"

—"My Uncle Terwilliger on the Art of Eating Popovers"

Think Before You Speak

My father had warned me, "Don't babble. Don't bray.
For you never can tell who might hear what you say."
My father had warned me, "Boy, button your lip."
And I guess that I should have. I made a bad slip.

—"Steak for Supper"

Tell the Truth

"Stop telling such outlandish tales.
Stop turning minnows into whales."

—*And to Think That I Saw It on Mulberry Street*

Respect Your Elders

You must not
hop on Pop.

—*Hop on Pop*

Focus!

This was no time for play.
This was no time for fun.
This was no time for games.
There was work to be done.

—*The Cat in the Hat Comes Back*

Don't Be Afraid to Accept Help

I floated twelve days without toothpaste or soap.
I practically, almost had given up hope
When someone up high shouted, "Here! Catch the rope!"
Then I knew that my troubles had come to an end
And I climbed up the rope, calling, "Thank you, my friend!"

—I Had Trouble in Getting to Solla Sollew

Expect the Unexpected

I heard a strange 'peep' and I took a quick look
And you know what I saw with the look that I took?
A bird laid an egg on my 'rithmetic book!

—"Marco Comes Late"

Face Up to Adversity

But I've bought a big bat.
I'm all ready, you see.
Now my troubles are going
To have troubles with *me*!

—I Had Trouble in Getting to Solla Sollew

Don't Obsess

This spot! It was driving me
 out of my mind!
What a spot—what a spot
 for a fellow to find!
My troubles were growing.
 The way it kept going!
Where would it go next?
 There was no way of knowing.

  —"The Strange Shirt Spot"

Be Careful

So I said to myself,
 "Now, I'll just have to start
To be twice as careful
 and be twice as smart.
I'll watch out for trouble
 in front and back sections
By aiming my eyeballs
 in different directions."

  —*I Had Trouble in Getting to Solla Sollew*

Try New Things

I do not like
green eggs
and ham!
I do not like them,
Sam-I-am.

You do not like them.
So you say.
Try them! Try them!
And you may.
Try them and you may, I say.

—*Green Eggs and Ham*

See the Light at the End of the Tunnel

Then, just when I thought I could stand it no more,
By chance I discovered a tiny trap door!
I popped my head out. The great sky was sky-blue
And I knew, from the flowers, I'd finally come through
To the banks of the beautiful River Wah-Hoo!

—I Had Trouble in Getting to Solla Sollew

Be Flexible

The bus stop was there. And that part was just fine.
But tacked on a stick was a very small sign
Saying, *"Notice to Passengers Using our Line:*
We are sorry to say that our driver, Butch Meyers,
Ran over four nails and has punctured all tires.
So, until further notice, the 4:42
Cannot possibly take you to Solla Sollew. . . .
But I wish you a most pleasant journey by feet.
Signed
Bus Line President, Horace P. Sweet."

—*I Had Trouble in Getting to Solla Sollew*

Take Chances

The places I hiked to!
  The roads that I rambled
To find the best eggs
  that have ever been scrambled! . . .
If you want to get eggs
  you can't buy at a store,
You have to do things
  never thought of before.

—*Scrambled Eggs Super!*

Expand Your Horizons

The more that you read,
the more things you will know.
The more that you learn,
the more places you'll go.

—I Can Read with My Eyes Shut!

Keep Your Eyes on the Prize

There are
so many things
you can learn about.
BUT . . . you'll miss
the best things
if you keep
your eyes shut.

—*I Can Read with My Eyes Shut!*

Embrace the Mysteries of Life

'Cause you never can tell
What goes on down below!
This pool *might* be bigger
Than you or I know!

—*McElligot's Pool*

Brainstorm

"Think! Think!" she cried.
Her Thinker-Upper gave a snorty snore.
It started thunk-thunk-thunking
As it never had before.
With all her might, her eyes shut tight,
She cried, "Thunk-thunk some more!"

—"The Glunk That Got Thunk"

Study

You can learn about ice.
You can learn about mice. . . .
You can learn about
the price of ice. . . .
You might learn
a way to earn
a few dollars.
Or how to make doughnuts . . .
or kangaroo collars.

—*I Can Read with My Eyes Shut!*

Make a Plan

Do you ever sit and fidget
when you don't know what to do . . . ?
Everybody gets the fidgets.
Even me and even you.

—*Hunches in Bunches*

Go the Extra Mile

So you see!
There's no end
To the things you might know,
Depending how far beyond Zebra you go!

—*On Beyond Zebra!*

Think Outside the Box

And ZATZ is the letter
   I use to spell Zatz-it
Whose nose is so high
   that 'most nobody pats it. . . .
So, to get there and do it,
   I built an invention:
The Three-Seater Zatz-it
   Nose-Patting Extension.

          —*On Beyond Zebra!*

Work Hard and Play Hard

But it's hard work being King,
and he does his work well.
If he wants to have a bit of fun . . .
sure! . . . let him have it!

—*The King's Stilts*

Be Grateful

When you think things are bad,
when you feel sour and blue,
when you start to get mad . . .
you should do what *I* do!
Just tell yourself, Duckie,
you're really quite lucky!
Some people are much more . . .
oh, ever so much more . . .
oh, muchly much-much more
unlucky than you!

—*Did I Ever Tell You How Lucky You Are?*

Put Your Best Foot Forward

Left foot
Right foot
Feet
Feet
Feet
How many, many
feet you meet.

—*The Foot Book*

Embrace Your Strengths

Shout loud, "I am lucky to be what I am!
Thank goodness I'm not just a clam or a ham
Or a dusty old jar of sour gooseberry jam!
I am what I am! That's a great thing to be!"

—*Happy Birthday to You!*

Be Proud of Who You Are

Of all
the shapes
we MIGHT have been . . .
I say, "HOORAY
for the shapes we're in!"

—*The Shape of Me and Other Stuff*

Be Proactive

UNLESS someone like you
cares a whole awful lot,
nothing is going to get better.
It's not.

—*The Lorax*

Go Green

Plant a new Truffula. Treat it with care.
Give it clean water. And feed it fresh air.
Grow a forest. Protect it from axes that hack.
Then the Lorax
and all of his friends
may come back.

—*The Lorax*

Check Out the Competition

You have to be smart and keep watching their feet.
Because sometimes they stand on their tiptoes and cheat.

—Happy Birthday to You!

Remain Humble

The rabbit felt mighty
    important that day
On top of the hill
    in the sun where he lay.
He felt SO important
    up there on that hill
That he started in bragging,
    as animals will . . .

—"The Big Brag"

Be Patient

"If I wait long enough;
    if I'm patient and cool,
Who knows *what* I'll catch
    in McElligot's Pool!"

—*McElligot's Pool*

Multitask

I can hold up the cup
And the milk and the cake!
I can hold up these books!
And the fish on a rake!
I can hold the toy ship
And a little toy man!
And look! With my tail
I can hold a red fan!
I can fan with the fan
As I hop on the ball!
But that is not all.
Oh, no.
That is not all. . . .

—*The Cat in the Hat*

Learn to Improvise

"All I need is a reindeer. . . ."
The Grinch looked around.
But, since reindeer are scarce, there was none to be found.
Did that stop the old Grinch . . . ?
No! The Grinch simply said,
"If I can't *find* a reindeer, I'll *make* one instead!"
So he called his dog, Max. Then he took some red thread
And he tied a big horn on the top of his head.

—*How the Grinch Stole Christmas!*

Think Big

My New Zoo, McGrew Zoo,
   will make people talk.
My New Zoo, McGrew Zoo,
   will make people gawk
At the strangest odd creatures
   that ever did walk.
I'll get, for my zoo,
   a new sort-of-a-hen
Who roosts in another hen's
   topknot, and *then*
Another one roosts
   in the topknot of his,
And another in *his,*
   and another in HIS,
And so forth and upward
   and onward, gee whizz!
       —*If I Ran the Zoo*

Don't Yell

I do not like
this one so well.
All he does
is yell, yell, yell.
I will not have this one about.
When he comes in
I put him out.

—*One Fish Two Fish Red Fish Blue Fish*

Treat Everyone as Your Equal

I'm quite happy to say
That the Sneetches got really quite smart on that day,
The day they decided that Sneetches are Sneetches
And no kind of Sneetch is the best on the beaches.

—"The Sneetches"

Remember the Little Guy

"It is good I have some one
To help me," he said.
"Right here in my hat
On the top of my head!
It is good that I have him
Here with me today.
He helps me a lot.
This is Little Cat A."

—*The Cat in the Hat Comes Back*

Pat Yourself on the Back

Come on! Open your mouth and sound off at the sky!
Shout loud at the top of your voice, "I AM I!
ME!
I am I!
And I may not know why
But I know that I like it.
Three cheers! I AM I!"

—*Happy Birthday to You!*

Take a Walk on the Wild Side

Did you ever
fly a kite
in bed?

Did you ever walk
with ten cats
on your head?

Did you ever milk
this kind of cow?
Well, we can do it.
We know how.
If you never did,
you should.
These things are fun
and fun is good.

—*One Fish Two Fish Red Fish Blue Fish*

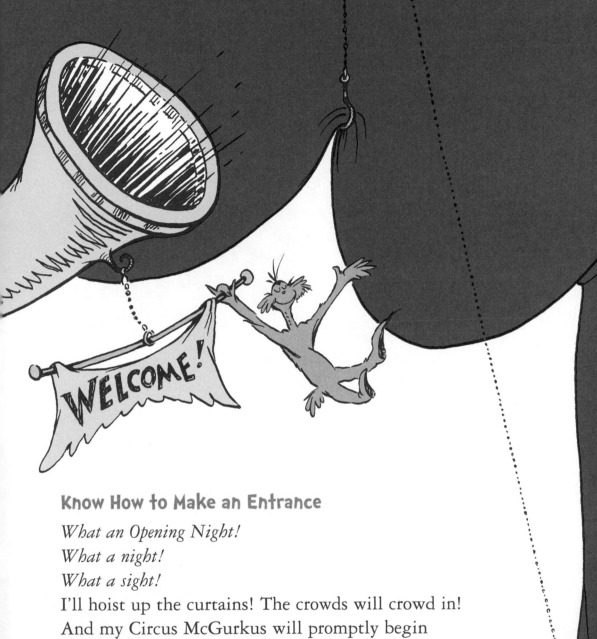

Know How to Make an Entrance

What an Opening Night!
What a night!
What a sight!
I'll hoist up the curtains! The crowds will crowd in!
And my Circus McGurkus will promptly begin
With a welcoming toot on my Welcoming Horn
By my horn-tooting apes from the Jungles of Jorn
Where the very best horn-tooting apes are all born
'Cause the very fresh air there is fine for their lungs.
And some of those fellows have two or three tongues!

—*If I Ran the Circus*

Be a Good Host

You couldn't say "Skat!" 'cause that wouldn't be right.
You couldn't shout "Scram!" 'cause that isn't polite.
A host has to put up with all kinds of pests,
For a host, above all, must be nice to his guests.
So you'd try hard to smile, and you'd try to look sweet
And you'd go right on looking for moose-moss to eat.

—Thidwick the Big-Hearted Moose

Know When to Call It a Night

Tomorrow will come.
    They'll go back to their chore.
They'll start on the road,
    Zizzer-Zoofing once more
But tonight they've forgotten
    their feet are so sore.
And that's what the wonderful
    night time is for.

—*Dr. Seuss's Sleep Book*

Indulge

I could eat a goose-moose burger,
fifteen pickles and a purple plum! . . .
Donuts, dumplings, blueberry bumplings,
choc'late mush-mush, super sweet.
Clam stew, ham stew, watermelon wush wush,
Oh, the things that I could eat!

—*The Cat in the Hat Songbook*

. . . But Don't Overindulge

Silly Sammy Slick
sipped six sodas
and got
sick sick sick.

—*Dr. Seuss's ABC*

Age Gracefully

You're in pretty good shape
for the shape you are in!

—*You're Only Old Once!*

Uphold Justice

I know, up on top
    you are seeing great sights,
But down at the bottom
    we, too, should have rights.

               —"Yertle the Turtle"

Let Freedom Ring

And the turtles, of course . . . all the turtles are free
As turtles and, maybe, all creatures should be.

               —"Yertle the Turtle"

Be Loyal

I meant what I said
And I said what I meant. . . .
An elephant's faithful
One hundred per cent!

—*Horton Hatches the Egg*

Cherish Diversity

We see them come.
We see them go.
Some are fast.
And some are slow.
Some are high.
And some are low.
Not one of them
is like another.
Don't ask us why.
Go ask your mother.

—*One Fish Two Fish Red Fish Blue Fish*

Never Underestimate the Power of One

A person's a person, no matter how small.

—*Horton Hears a Who!*

. . . Or the Power of Song

The Chief Yookeroo had sent them to meet me
along with the Right-Side-Up Song Girls to greet me.
They sang:
   "Oh, be faithful!
   Believe in thy butter!"
And they lifted my spirits right out of the gutter!

—*The Butter Battle Book*

Search for Meaning

Then the Grinch thought of something he hadn't before!
"Maybe Christmas," he thought, "*doesn't* come from a store.
Maybe Christmas . . . perhaps . . . means a little bit more!"

—*How the Grinch Stole Christmas!*

Open Your Heart

And what happened *then* . . . ?
Well . . . in *Who*-ville they say
That the Grinch's small heart
Grew three sizes that day!

—*How the Grinch Stole Christmas!*

And Always Remember

And will you succeed?
Yes! You will, indeed!
(98 and ¾ percent guaranteed.)
KID, YOU'LL MOVE MOUNTAINS!

—*Oh, the Places You'll Go!*

And Those Already on Their Way